BENJI FRANKLIN

KID ZILLIONAIRE

Stone Arch Books
a Capstone Imprint

Benji Franklin: Kid Zillionaire
is published by Stone Arch Books,
a Capstone Imprint
1710 Roe Crest Drive
North Mankato, Minnesota 56003
www.capstonepub.com

Cataloging-in-Publication Data is available on
the Library of Congress website.
ISBN: 978-1-4342-6417-6 (library hardcover)

Summary: After inventing a best-selling computer app,
Benjamin "Benji" Franklin becomes the world's only
ZILLIONAIRE. But this twelve-year-old tycoon knows
life isn't all about the Benjamin. He's planning to use his
newfound wealth for the greater good—like saving the
world from killer dinosaurs!

Graphic Designer: Brann Garvey
Creative Director: Heather Kindseth
Production Specialist: Laura Manthe

Printed in the United States of America in Stevens Point, Wisconsin.
092013   007765WZS14

BENJI FRANKLIN

KID ZILLIONAIRE

SAVING
MONEY
(and the World from Killer Dinos!)

written by
Raymond Bean

illustrated by
Matthew Vimislik

Table of Contents

CHAPTER 1

Mega-Sized Dreams

My name's Benjamin Franklin, but most people call me Benji. As you probably guessed, my parents named me after one of the most creative minds in history. Talk about pressure!

Benjamin Franklin — Brilliant

Benji Franklin — Kid

Right from the get-go, people had mega-sized dreams for me. Not to brag, but I didn't disappoint. At six months old, I learned sign language. When I was three, I taught myself how to play the guitar—acoustic, of course. At five, I was able to read in six different languages, including Dolphin (*EE-EEEK!*).

My mom thinks I'm brilliant, but I'm not so sure. Do true geniuses crave candy 24 hours a day?

A real genius, Albert Einstein, once said: "It's not that I'm so smart, it's just that I stay with problems longer." I feel the same way. It's not that I'm supersmart. I'm just really, REALLY curious!

Luckily, my dad and I share a ginormous workshop behind my house. It's a great place to create (...or break!) all kinds of stuff.

My grandpa built the workshop like a hundred years ago. Loads of his old cars, dusty boats, rusty motors, and other odd items still fill the rotting shed. If it flew, rolled, or floated, there's a good chance it's hiding in there somewhere.

My dad grew up tinkering with stuff, too. In fact, he's so good at building things that last year he created a satellite from a car radio, a spare tire, an aquarium, and the rear seat of a minivan.

A few weeks ago, we launched the satellite into space from our backyard. It. Was. AWESOME!

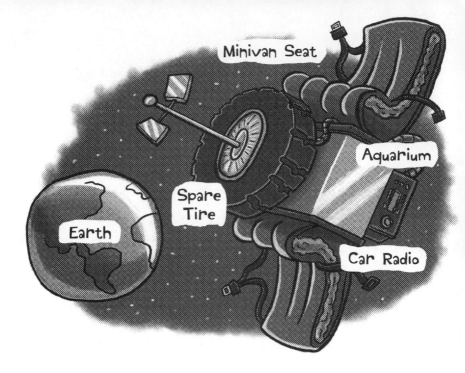

Kids at school didn't believe me when I told them about the satellite...until I showed them the FBI footage. (Don't ask!)

One day, while I downloaded data from the satellite, my dad rolled up on his rusty old motorcycle. "Your piano lesson starts in ten minutes," he said, taking off his helmet.

"But I'm tracking asteroids," I replied. "There's dozens of them whizzing by today!"

Dad walked over and peeked at the data. "How's the satellite looking?" he asked, adjusting his glasses.

"It'll be fine," I assured him. "It doesn't seem like any of the 'roids will take it out."

"That's good news," he said, opening the workshop door. "Because I have work to do!"

After reading a news article about a fisherman who fell overboard, Dad towed an old boat into our workshop. Then he started designing a safety system for fishing boats. His idea was to cover each crewmember's jacket, pants, and boots with thousands of tiny magnets and rig the fishing boat with a superpowered magnet. If a fisherman fell in the water, the magnet could pull him back to the boat safely.

"How's the suit coming?" I asked.

"I'm ready for a test, Benji," he said, putting on one of the magnetic jackets. "Climb into the boat with me, will you? Let's see if this gizmo is strong enough to pull me back in!"

"Are you sure it's safe to test?" I asked.

"Nope! But there's only one way to find out." Dad leaped off the boat and onto the shed floor below. "Man overboard!" he cried out.

I flipped the safety switch. Instead of being pulled toward the ship, he shot away from it as if he'd been fired out of a cannon. **WHAM!!** He blasted through the old shed like a human wrecking ball.

I quickly jumped off the boat and ran up to the hole in the wall.

"Are you all right, Dad?" I asked, worried.

"Yep! Guess I had the magnets reversed," he said. "When you flipped the switch, they repelled instead of attracted me. If the attraction is that strong, I think this idea just might work, son."

"Benji! Your piano teacher is here!" I heard Mom shout from the house.

"Do I have to go, Dad?" I asked.

"You know the drill, kiddo. Piano is great for the mind," he said. "It helps develop your synapses."

"What if my synapses don't want developing?"

"As much as I'd like for you to stay here and give me a hand, you've got to go," he replied.

"But...what if I had a terrible headache?" I asked, holding my forehead.

"You'd have to go straight to bed and maybe the doctor," he said.

"But...what if—" I began.

"Benji, what if you stopped trying to excuse yourself?" he said. "Go tickle those ivories."

CHAPTER 2
Excuse Yourself

Weeks earlier, my tech teacher, Mrs. Heart, had assigned a class project. Each student in the class had to create a computer app that people would want to buy.

When Dad said, "What if you stopped trying to excuse yourself?," an idea hit me like an asteroid. Kids all over the world try getting out of BORING stuff every day. They make up endless excuses to avoid the chores they don't want to do.

What if I created an app to help kids get out of these tasks? I wondered. *Like piano lessons!*

I even thought of an app name...Excuse Yourself!

I could hardly concentrate during my piano lesson. I kept thinking about my grandfather. He used to say that his greatest ideas always came to him in a flash.

"Brilliance strikes like lightning!" he'd tell me. "One minute it's not there, and the next—**BOOM!**—an idea flashes across the sky. You can't miss it."

The Excuse Yourself computer app was a brilliant idea. I knew that much instantly.

After a few days, the app worked just the way I wanted it. I'd taught myself how to write computer code when I was younger, and the skill really came in handy. Mrs. Heart had taught us a few useful tricks in class to help create an app, but most of the cooler features I had figured out on my own.

The day the app was due, I realized most of the kids in my class had created *games*. As my time to present neared, I could hardly contain my excitement. A few kids presented before me, and then Mrs. Heart called me to the front of the class.

I stood in front of the large digital board. "How many of you have made up an excuse to get yourself out of trouble?" I asked.

Every hand went up. *Perfect!* I thought.

"Of course you have," I continued. "We all make excuses, and even lie from time to time. But what if I told you there was an app that helps you get out of trouble? Raise your hand if you'd use it."

Again, every hand went up.

This time though, when the hands went back down, one person's remained up—Cindy Meyers's.

Cindy never raised her hand unless she wanted to complain about something. "Do you want to say something, Cindy?" I asked, cautiously.

"If you're talking about an excuse app, Benji, save your breath," she said. "It's been done." She pointed to another app on her cellphone.

"You're right," I agreed. "Plenty of excuse apps already exist, but none like the one I've created!"

I tapped the digital board, and my computer app launched. The words "Excuse Yourself" appeared on the screen's homepage.

"Clever name, Benji!" the teacher exclaimed.

"Thanks, Mrs. Heart," I said. "Like it's name, the Excuse Yourself app is anything but ordinary. If you need an excuse, simply type your question into the powerful search engine." I scrolled through the app's menu bar, demonstrating for the class.

"Like other apps, Excuse Yourself gives you dozens of possible excuses," I explained. "But, unlike the competition, my computer app helps you determine the likelihood the excuse will work! Someone give me an example of something you needed an excuse for today."

A kid named Mark raised his hand. "I got in trouble last period," he said. "I didn't read the book Mr. Frayne assigned."

"Fantastic!" I said. Then I typed: **Didn't read the book I was supposed to read for class.**

The app immediately created a list of excuses:

EXCUSE	ODDS OF WORKING
Lost it.	30%
Family emergency.	85%
Book made me cry.	80%
Read the book; couldn't understand it.	67%
Received eye drops at doctor; can't see.	98%
Headache/stomachache/ache of any kind.	25%
More options...	

The class seemed interested.

"That's not all," I continued. "Once I've made my selection, the app will advise me of the possible challenges I may encounter if I decide to use this excuse. Which one do you want to use, Mark?"

"The eye drops," he replied. "That's a new one."

I clicked on the fifth option: **Received eye drops at doctor; can't see.**

The app generated a list of advice for the user:

· **May need a note.**

· **School nurse may call or e-mail home to confirm.**

· **Teacher may ask, "What's wrong?" Say you don't know the name of the condition; a kid wouldn't remember something like that.**

· **Rub your eyes, but don't overdo it.**

"That's awesome!" Mark said.

"Hold on. The app goes one step further, " I said. "Most kids use the same excuse over and over. I've added a feature that tracks when you've used excuses and who you've used them on." Again, I demonstrated the feature on screen.

"Also, the app keeps a record of all your excuse activity," I explained. "If someone asks you about an excuse you gave a few weeks back, there's no need to remember the details. Simply click your excuse history, and it's all there for you."

You could've heard a pin drop in the classroom. The other students' minds were spinning with possibilities. My teacher chewed her bottom lip and tried to force a smile.

A few kids had their cell phones out. They were hiding them under the desks, so Mrs. Heart wouldn't notice. I thought it was pretty rude that they were playing on their phones, and I hadn't even finished my presentation!

Mrs. Heart interrupted. "I just want to be clear, Benji. Are you encouraging kids to lie?"

"No, ma'am!" I exclaimed. "Honesty is the best policy, of course. I'm saying that, like it or not, we all tell fibs from time to time. My Excuse Yourself app helps once someone has already made the decision to make an excuse."

"That stills sounds a lot like lying," she said.

"Kids already do a lot of lying on their own," I argued. "And that brings me to one final feature, which I'm very proud of."

I felt like a salesman on a TV infomercial. I was really selling it! "Excuse Yourself provides users with graphs, data, and charts to help them understand how often they make excuses," I explained. "Kids might actually learn about their behavior and maybe even change." Mrs. Heart had to like that part, even though she was unsure about the app.

"Very imaginative," said Mrs. Heart. "I just wanted to make sure you weren't encouraging lying in order to get out of responsibility."

"It's AWESOME, Franklin!" Mark said again.

"Yes, Mark," Mrs. Heart said. "It is awesome, but it still concerns me a bit. You kids shouldn't actually use the Excuse Yourself app. It's simply a fun idea."

"Can I buy it?" asked Mark, ignoring her.

"It's available online," I replied. "But, like Mrs. Heart said, the app's not really for everyday use. It's more of a goof than anything else."

$ $ $

That night, I helped Dad in the workshop with the deep-sea safety gear. The magnets were working much better. When he flipped the switch, the magnets pulled me across the floor. The invention wasn't ready to pull a grown man out of the ocean, but it was getting closer.

After that, we tracked some debris approaching our satellite, and then we headed to pick Mom up from the food pantry where she volunteers.

When we arrived, she was organizing cans of food and placing them on shelves.

"I'm about ready to go," she said. "I just want to drop a care package off to a family on the way."

"No problem," Dad said.

She grabbed me by the hand. "Come with me, Benjamin. You can help carry a few more things."

Mom has volunteered at the food pantry so long that she practically runs the place. She handed me an empty bag and walked toward the fridges.

"Grab two containers of milk and some butter," she said to me. "I'll meet you back at the front."

I opened the large, silver refrigerator doors and walked inside. It was FREEZING! I saw some chicken, eggs, and butter, but no milk. I grabbed the items and headed back to the front to meet Mom.

"You're out of milk," I told her.

"Again?" she said with a sigh. "I can't seem to keep it on the shelves. We'll have to stop on the way and pick some up."

"We'd better go," Dad said. "It looks like rain."

"Please tell me you didn't bring that ridiculous motorcycle," Mom groaned.

"I didn't bring that *ridiculous* motorcycle," Dad said, smirking. He turned to me and whispered, "It's not ridiculous."

"Uh-huh," Mom said. "Then I'm driving. Benji, you can sit in the sidecar with your father."

"Not AGAIN!" Dad cried.

Dad got funny looks from people when he drove the motorcycle. But when Mom was driving with Dad and me in the sidecar...people died laughing!

$ $ $

We stopped to buy milk and then dropped the supplies off for a family. I was surprised that there were two kids playing out in front of the house when we pulled up. I'd been to the pantry with Mom many times, but I'd never seen the families she helped in person. The mother hugged my mom. It was clear that Mom had been there many times before. She introduced us to the woman and her kids.

"Your mother is one of the most generous people I've ever known," said the woman.

"I just like to help," said Mom.

"You're an amazing person," the woman added.

"You guys take care of yourselves," Mom told them. "Remember, let me know if you need anything at all."

The woman teared up as we left. I never knew how much Mom's work helped people.

Later that night, I was setting the table for dinner. "How would those people have fed their kids if you didn't bring them all that stuff?" I asked.

"I'm not sure, Benji," she replied.

"How come you guys were out of milk?" I asked.

"We operate on donations, so we only have what people give us," Mom explained. "Today, there wasn't enough milk, so I decided to buy it."

"How often do you buy the stuff yourself?"

"More often than you'd think," she said. "We get a bunch of food around the holidays, but the rest of the year is pretty tough. Working on donations alone just isn't sustainable. We're always running out of things and people go hungry."

"Isn't there a better way to help people that need food?" I said.

"When you figure it out," she said. "I'm all ears."

CHAPTER 3

My First Million

The next morning was Saturday. I logged into the bank account I'd created for my app. I figured a few kids in my class might have bought it. Maybe I'd have enough money to buy some candy (YUM!).

I clicked my balance and couldn't believe my eyes! When I left for school Friday, my account was at $1.39 because I'd bought the app myself to make

sure it worked. The app sold for $1.99 online. Every time someone bought it, $1.39 went straight to my new bank account.

I was expecting ten dollars or so, but the balance was...$344,052!

CHA-CHING!!

I got out my calculator and divided the balance by $1.39. If my math was correct (and why wouldn't it be!), the app had been downloaded nearly 250,000 times. Overnight!

This must be a mistake, I thought. I refreshed the page, expecting the number to return to something like ten cents. But instead...

$353,060!

CHA-CHING!!

Could that many people have downloaded the app in only a few seconds? I clicked it a third time, and the number went up again!

By the time I called my parents into my room, the account was even higher. The numbers were changing so rapidly that it reminded me of numbers on the gas pump when Dad fills the tank. They were spinning too fast to even make out the digits.

"You didn't hack into a bank or anything, did you?" Dad asked, warily.

"Of course he didn't hack into a bank. Don't be ridiculous," Mom said. "You didn't, did you?"

"No!"

"The Federal Reserve?" Dad asked.

"Remember that computer app I created for tech class?" I asked.

"The last time you mentioned it, you were stuck for ideas," Dad replied.

"Right! But I got an idea when I was trying to get out of my piano lesson the other day," I explained. "I built an app and presented it to the class yesterday. I put it up for sale on the app store, but I didn't expect people to actually buy it."

"This is all from a computer app?" Mom asked. "How can you make this much selling an app?"

"It's going viral!" Dad exclaimed, sitting at my desk to have a closer look at the data.

"This thing is being downloaded all over the world," he said. "What does it do, Benji?"

"It makes excuses," I said, anticipating a reaction from my mom.

"Why doesn't the number stop spinning?" Mom asked. "It just keeps getting bigger."

"Because it's being downloaded so often," Dad said. "Every time someone buys the app, the number goes up. This is amazing! I've never seen anything like it."

"What does this thing do again?" Mom asked.

"It's called Excuse Yourself," I repeated softly.

"How wonderful!" said Mom, giving me a big smile. "So it teaches young people good manners?"

"Uh...not exactly," I said.

She gave me a stony stare. "You better show me how it works."

$ $ $

When Mom downloaded the app to her phone, she clicked around silently for a few minutes. She didn't look too happy.

"I'm not sure this is appropriate, Benjamin," she said. "All these people are using your app to get out of trouble. They're lying!"

"They're not really lying, Mom," I assured her.

"Actually, they are," she said. "You've given people a way of getting out of responsibilities in a dishonest way. Last time I checked, *that* was lying."

"People lie all the time, Mom," I said. "They don't ever really think about how often they're doing it. Maybe it will help people see the amount of excuses they're making and change?"

"Nice try, kiddo," she said. "Why couldn't you have created something more useful and positive?"

"Mrs. Heart told us we had to create an app that people would want to buy," I replied. "I didn't expect it to go beyond my classroom."

"Hmmm."

"I was just having fun with it, Mom," I added. "Who would have thought it would be this popular?"

"Hey, check this out!" Dad interrupted. "Benji's app is being discussed all over the Internet."

He was right.

The app *had* gone viral.

Bloggers and websites all over the globe were writing about it. Some people were saying how great it was. Others were really angry about the idea.

We silently read several of the articles and tried to grasp what was happening.

"I think we should have breakfast and give this a little time to process," Dad said. "I haven't even had a chance to look at this miraculous new creation."

We all sat at the kitchen table. Mom and Dad each played with Excuse Yourself. After several moments of silence, Dad said, "I won't be able to mow the lawn this weekend because I'm suffering from seasonal allergies."

"You don't have allergies!" Mom said, focusing on the app.

"Then, I can't mow the lawn because I twisted my ankle yesterday," he said, giving me a wink. "It still feels a little tender."

Mom picked up on what he was doing. "Very cute, honey," she said. "Your ankle is fine, and I wish I could say the same for your son's app."

"I think it's interesting," Dad said, hesitantly.

"And inappropriate," Mom added.

"I don't know if I'd say 'inappropriate,'" Dad responded. "But it's definitely controversial."

"Our son has basically created a database of lies people can use to get out of work," she said.

"True, but it's up to the individual to decide if they're going to use an excuse or not." Dad continued to defend me. "Once they click on the site, they've already made the decision to find an excuse. Benji didn't have anything to do with that."

Dad held his bowl of cereal in the air. "A chef can't be blamed for the customer's hunger," he said.

Dad added, "The customer is already hungry. The chef only provides the food."

"Benji isn't cooking *food*," said Mom. He's cooking up *lies*. We've got a real problem here."

"Guys," I interrupted.

"Yes?" Mom asked, annoyed.

"I'm sorry to interrupt," I said, "but I might have just become a MILLIONAIRE!!"

NET INCOME:
$1,000,000

CHAPTER 4
Zillionaire?

The week that followed was *completely* insane! Every news show, magazine, blog, and tech company wanted to meet me. One company even offered me a job, but we would've had to move to California, and Dad has a fear of earthquakes.

I couldn't believe they'd offered a kid my age a job. My parents and I did interviews, took phone calls, and tried our best to manage all the attention.

My parents were most excited for all the interviews and talk shows. Especially the interview with the news show *Your World with Chuck Matthews*. They watch it every Sunday night and were thrilled to be on the show. We did the interview on Saturday afternoon. It was on that show's interview that Mom's concerns about honesty were really put to the test.

"Are you worried that your son, Benji, has created an app that helps people lie?" Chuck Matthews asked Mom.

Mom froze, but just for a nanosecond. "Well, Mr. Matthews, that's a question Benjamin and I have discussed a great deal," she replied. "We're hopeful that Excuse Yourself is a place where people—"

"What are your plans for the money your son is making?" interrupted Chuck Matthews.

"We're adjusting to it," said Dad. "For now, life for Benjamin will remain the same as it always—"

"I hear you have a golden submarine," said Chuck, turning to me.

"Two of them, actually," I replied. "The first one sank, so I had to buy a second one to go down and rescue the crew."

"And you have a private island?" asked Chuck.

I waved my hand. "Just a small one, Chuck," I said. "Although I have applied for nation status."

My mom tried to change the subject. "Uh, we feel the app is a good way for Benjamin to connect with the world," she said.

"Yes," chimed in Dad. "It's a way to connect more positively and—"

"What's this I hear about a space station?" asked Chuck, looking directly at me.

"Space is where it's at, Chuck," I said. "And it's a great place to keep my zoo."

Benji Franklin
"Kid Zillionaire"

Your World
with
Chuck Matthews

"Your zoo?" he said.

"I was running out of room on the island," I said. "Those Tibetan yaks take up a lot more room than you'd think."

"You have yaks?" asked Chuck.

"For the milk," I said. "It's very healthy."

Then Chuck stared out at his studio audience and said, "I bet I'd like some of that. You know how much I like to *yak*!"

The audience went wild. They cheered and laughed and even clapped.

Chuck sat back in his chair and smiled at me. I could tell the interview was going well. "So," he said at last, "you're a sixth-grade zillionaire?"

"A zillion isn't a real number," I pointed out.

"True," said Chuck, nodding. "But what else do you call a kid with more money than he can count?"

"Generous," said my mother quickly.

"Thoughtful," said my father.

"Lucky," I said. "And very excited about my new space station."

CHAPTER 5
Greater Good

The next morning, we got a mysterious call from a man named Dr. Snow. Dad talked to him for a while, and then he handed me the phone. I figured it was another interview, or another celebrity, or another pro athlete who wanted to hang out.

"Hi, Benji," a voice on the other end said. "I'm a researcher and founder of the B.A.D.R. Institute. I've been following your story. We have a situation here at the Institute that we feel you might be able to assist with. Are you free to come out and meet us tomorrow night?"

"Hmm, I don't know," I said. "Where are you located? Can I get there by nuclear sub?"

"Uh, no."

"Can I get there by solar-powered rocket ship?"

"No."

"Can I get there by dogsled pulled by twelve Olympic athletes?" (I can pay for all those things, by the way.)

"No."

"Wow!" I said. "You guys must be hidden in some supersecret faraway exotic location!"

"We're fifteen miles down the road," he said.

"Oh," I said.

"Our situation is rather dire," said the man. "We need to meet in person."

"I'm a kid," I explained, although I'm sure he already knew. "I have school. Which is also dire. You'll have to work out the details with my dad."

I yawned and handed the phone to Dad, and he walked off with it.

Saying "I'm a kid" is an excuse that I came up with on my app. It works in almost every situation with adults.

"What was that all about?" Mom asked.

"I don't know," I said. "They wanted to talk with me about a problem they have."

"I think this app is just the beginning of big things for you, Benjamin," she said. "Promise me you won't lose sight of who you are."

"I promise," I assured her. "Nothing has really changed if you think about it. Well, maybe my clothes. And the private island and stuff. Otherwise, all that's happened is a bunch of people are downloading the app."

"When things settle down, we'll have to sort out what we're going to do with all that money," said Mom. "I hope you don't forget that it's not all about the Benjamins, Benjamin."

"What does that mean?" I asked. I couldn't help smirking a bit because Mom was trying to be cool.

"Isn't that what people call large sums of money?" she asked. "Don't they say that in movies?"

"They do," I said. "And you don't have to worry. I know it's not all about the Benjamins, Mom."

"There are things in the world that matter more than money," she said. "You saw for yourself the other day how that family was in need."

"I know, Mom."

"Did you know I read this morning about an entire town that is in need?" she said.

"How does that happen?" I asked.

"They live in a town called Shiny Desert," she explained. "It's way out in the middle of nowhere."

Mom continued. "The people who live there went for work because a big computer company built its offices out there. They wanted to develop their product in complete secrecy. These people worked there for years and, all of a sudden, the company went out of business. There's nothing else there, but the people in the town can't afford to move away."

"Can your pantry help them?" I asked.

"We've sent what we can," she said. "Other pantries are sending what they can as well, but the town is in big trouble. They're in the middle of the desert. There's nothing around for miles."

"Let's donate some of the money from Excuse Yourself to help them out," I said.

"I might just ask you to do that," she said. "For now, you just make sure the next thing you invent does more than just get people out of trouble. Think about the greater good."

The greater good? That would be a cool name for an app.

"I won't be inventing anything new for a while, Mom," I said. "Besides, I have school tomorrow!"

CHAPTER 6
B.A.D.R. Institute

Fifteen miles from my house was the site of an old airport. I'd always thought the buildings there were abandoned, but it was where the B.A.D.R. Institute was located.

Late the next night, my dad drove me out to meet Dr. Snow. "What do you think they want?" I shouted over the roar of the motorcycle.

"Who knows?" Dad said. "That scientist said he'd have to explain when we got there."

"It's a little strange that they want to meet at ten o'clock at night, don't you think?" I asked. "I researched them on the computer, and I couldn't find anything. It's a little weird."

Dad shrugged. "If it's weird, we'll leave," he said. "No biggie."

When we arrived, a security guard stood at the entrance to the facility. Dad explained who we were and who we were there to see. The guard's eye twitched a few times. He looked behind him, shining his flashlight toward the woods.

"Everything okay?" Dad asked.

"That depends," the guard replied.

"On what?" I asked.

"On your definition of 'okay,'" he replied.

"I'm not sure what you mean," Dad said.

"You will soon enough," the guard said. "Dr. Snow and the others are in building seven, all the way in the back. It's the only one with a light on."

The guard turned his attention to the woods. "They're waiting for you."

$ $ $

When we rolled up, Dr. Snow was waiting for us outside. He was much, much, much older looking than I'd expected. Maybe TWICE as old as Dad.

"Mr. Franklin," Dr. Snow said, as I climbed out of the sidecar. I figured he was talking to my dad until he walked toward me, holding his hand out for a handshake. "Pleasure to meet you."

I shook his hand and noticed he was glancing toward the woods like the security guard.

"Come on," he said. "We'd better get inside."

Inside, a large oval table sat in the center of a massive room. The room looked like an old hangar for airplanes. It had a really high ceiling. There were about twenty people sitting around the table. They

looked about the same age as Dr. Snow.

Dr. Snow introduced us to the group and asked us to have a seat.

"I have to say, this is a little strange. Benji and I are a bit confused about why we're here," Dad said.

"Understood," Dr. Snow said, clicking a button on his phone. A large screen lowered from the ceiling and the lights dimmed. "Mr. Franklin, we've been following your story. We read the articles about you and think it's amazing that a local kid is receiving so much attention for his intellect. You're clearly very creative, and we think you can help us out. Unfortunately, we find ourselves in a particularly sensitive situation."

I couldn't remember a time in my life when people were so nice to me. Kids usually gave me a hard time because I'm smart. When I was really young, sometimes I pretended to be confused in class just to fit in with the others. Something was changing though. I felt more proud of being smart and not as embarrassed.

"Who are you guys?" I asked. "I couldn't find anything online about the B.A.D.R. Institute."

"Our work is top secret and privately funded," said Dr. Snow. "Few people know what we do."

"What does your name stand for?" Dad asked.

"It stands for Bio Advancement of Dinosaur Research Institute," the scientist explained.

"Before I tell you the specifics," he continued, "I'll have to ask you sign this paper stating that you won't share any of the details we tell you tonight. We'll have to ask you to sign as well, Mr. Franklin." He turned toward my dad.

Dad nodded to me, and we both signed.

"Very well," Dr. Snow said, collecting the papers. "Do you know what a Troodon dinosaur is?"

"Hmm...didn't they star in the movie *Jurassic Park*?" I said.

"We recently obtained rare samples of Troodon DNA," he continued. "To make a long story short, we've managed to clone them."

He clicked his remote and a holographic image of a dinosaur appeared above us.

"You have living dinosaurs!" I exclaimed.

"You could say that," a woman across the larger table said. From the expression on Dr. Snow's face, I could tell he didn't like the woman very much.

"We don't have to get into all the specifics, Professor Kent," Dr. Snow said, interrupting.

"If he's going to help, doctor, he's going to need all the details. We don't have much time," Dr. Kent replied.

"How does all this involve Benji?" Dad asked.

"As I hinted on the phone last night, we have a situation," said Dr. Snow.

"Good grief! Just come out with it already," Dr. Kent shouted. "The Troodon escaped!"

"We have, um, misplaced them," Dr. Snow corrected her.

"They're out of their pens, and we haven't seen them in forty-eight hours! They're probably still in the woods behind the Institute, but there's no way to be sure," Dr. Kent added.

I was still trying to fully comprehend that they had living dinosaurs on the loose. The room was silent, and they were all looking at me.

"I'm not sure what you guys want me for," I said.

"You created Excuse Yourself. If there's anyone who can think of a way out of this situation, it's you," Dr. Snow said.

Dr. Snow seemed really worried to me in that moment. It was like he was a kid that got in trouble and couldn't get himself out. Dr. Kent acted a little like his mother (although she obviously wasn't!).

"You realize I created that app in my sixth-grade tech class?" I said. "I'm not a scientist or anything."

"Yes, but you're an expert in creating excuses," said Dr. Snow. "We need several if we're going to keep this from the public. Do you know what will happen if people learn prehistoric beasts are roaming around the city?"

"I can't imagine they'll be too happy," Dad said.

Dr. Kent added, "Benji, catching these dinosaurs isn't going to be easy. They're highly intelligent, and the land behind our facility extends for miles. If we don't catch them soon, and they make contact with people, we're going to have a much bigger problem on our hands."

Dr. Snow agreed. "We have to catch them in a way that no one knows this little mishap ever took place," he said. "We want to continue to study the Troodon in secrecy at another location. If the public learns about their existence, we'll never have peace again, and the Troodon will be doomed."

I didn't want to be rude or anything, but I had to ask. "I hope you guys don't take this the wrong way, but if you were clever enough to figure out how to clone live dinosaurs, shouldn't you be able to figure out a way to catch them without my help?"

"*We* didn't clone them, Benji," Dr. Kent shared. "Dr. Snow, who happens to be very wealthy, paid the world's leading biologists to clone the Troodon."

"Once the dinosaurs escaped," she said, "the scientists were afraid of getting in trouble, so they bailed out. They left us to clean up the mess."

"So if you hired scientists to do the work, what are you guys?" I asked.

"We're paleontologists, Benji," said Dr. Snow. "We know a lot about dinosaur bones and their history, but not a whole lot about how to handle them if they're alive."

"You're young enough to appreciate the dinosaurs, Benji," added Dr. Kent. "We're afraid that if we share our situation with adults, they'll want to capitalize on it and make money. We just want to catch the Troodon safely and continue our research, not exploit them or cause them any more harm. It's got to be you. You may be our only hope."

CHAPTER 7
The Troodon Solution

Sometimes when I'm solving a problem, my mind takes over, and I can't hear anything else around me. It happens when I solve puzzles and complex problems. My mind visualizes the solution one piece at a time. I see a bunch of different images in my head. The images swirl around in my

mind, independent of one another. If I concentrate hard enough, I can always find a way that they connect together to make a solution.

My mother says that when I was really young, I used to call this process chicken-and-idea soup!

Even today, when I get in a deep concentration while solving a problem, my parents say I'm making soup. It was happening at the table. I was completely zoned out.

I was aware that Dad and the scientist were still talking, but I was too lost in my thoughts to hear what they were saying. There were so many things running through my mind at once that it was hard to keep up. I envisioned myself capturing the Troodon and sending them somewhere safe. My mother was there. We were standing in a field, and she was really proud of me. In that moment, it all clicked.

"I see it!" I said, snapping out of my haze.

"You see the Troodon?" asked Dr. Kent, turning around quickly.

"A solution," I said. "I think I can solve your problem, but I'm going to need a few things first."

"Just like that? You've figured out a solution?" Dr. Kent asked.

"What will you need?" Dr. Snow asked.

I grabbed a pen and a sheet of paper from the table and wrote out my list. It was like a dream. I knew that if I didn't write everything down, I might forget something important:

15,000 Square feet of clear, high-security glass

1 Remote-control helicopter with video camera

1 Crew of carpenters/painters

1 Crane

1 Large flatbed truck

$6 million dollars in cash

75 –100 Dairy cows

150 –200 Chickens

I slid the note across the table to Dr. Snow. "Chickens?" he said. "You need chickens and cows?"

"We'll need them if we're going to do this right," I said. "It's not for me. It's for the greater good."

"This will be expensive," said Dr. Snow.

"Brain power isn't cheap," I said, acting confident.

"And you can guarantee that no one will learn of the Troodon?" Dr. Kent asked.

"Unless someone here tells people about it," I said, "I guarantee it."

"Can you guarantee the safety of those chickens as well?" she added.

"I'm not prepared to answer that at this point."

"Personally, I'm not so sure you've even cloned a dinosaur successfully," Dad said, challenging them a bit. "No offense, it's just I'm a man of science. I haven't seen any evidence so far to lead me to think this is a real problem you have here."

"Oh, I wish we were making this up, Mr. Franklin," Dr. Kent said. "You'll see soon enough, the Troodon are quite real."

"Well, that's what I'll need if I'm going to capture them. I can do it quickly, and no one will ever know this happened," I said. "You'll have your solution and an excuse for any commotion we might cause."

"You've got a deal," Dr. Snow said.

A younger man who'd been sitting quietly across the table said, "Let's hear how the kid plans to capture the Troodon." The lack of white in his hair meant he was the youngest one in the room, except for me of course.

"I don't want to know, Professor Clive," Dr. Snow said. "If the Troodon damage or hurt someone, it'll cost us far more than what Benji is asking. I'll order the materials right away. We'll send you a bill when the Troodon are all bolted safely back in their enclosures."

"Well, in that case, what are we sitting around here talking for?" I asked. "I don't know about you, Dad, but I want to see a living dinosaur!"

"That makes two of us," he said.

$ $ $

Young Dr. Clive insisted the other scientists wait in building seven. He took Dad and I to the hangar.

We walked for several minutes down a long, narrow trail behind the buildings that led to a clearing. "Was this the old runway when this place was an airport?" I asked, glancing out into the darkness.

"Yep," Dr. Clive replied, pointing at an old airplane hangar on the far side of the clearing. The farther we walked, I could hear a high-pitched screeching.

"Is that—?" I started to ask.

"Yes, Benji," he replied. "That is the sound of a living dinosaur."

Inside the hangar, there was only a three-foot wide space to stand in. The rest of the room was enclosed in a glass cage that rose all the way to the ceiling. "They're nocturnal, you know, so she should be pretty active," said Dr. Clive.

It was dark inside, except for the moonlight coming through the window. My eyes took a few seconds to adjust.

Dr. Clive gripped my arm and turned me toward the farthest corner of the hangar. He pointed. The Troodon stood so still that if I didn't know better I would have thought it was a statue.

The beast stood about fifteen feet from us and was a little taller than me. We were as silent as possible. I didn't even breathe. It shrieked, causing the hair on the back of my neck to stand up and my skin to tingle with excitement.

"Unbelievable!" I whispered to Dad.

"Totally," he whispered back.

"I wonder how much she'd cost," I said.

"Is that enough proof for you, Mr. Franklin?" Dr. Clive asked.

"Yes, sir," Dad and I answered at the same time.

I couldn't look away. The Troodon had a long, thin head and an even thinner neck. It reminded me of a mini *T. rex*. The skin was like a lizard's. It was muscular and stood on two legs like an ostrich.

"That's the coolest thing I've ever seen!" I said.

"It's also the most insanely dangerous thing you may ever encounter," Dr. Clive warned. "Don't take these beasts lightly, young man. They're brighter than you might imagine."

"They must be clever if they managed to get out of here," I said, looking around the enclosure.

"They had one of the largest brains in the dinosaur world," explained Dr. Clive.

"You must mean *have*," said Dad. I was wondering how to transport the Troodon to my space station zoo.

"Dr. Snow thought he'd be able to bring them back and train them to be pets."

"Looks like they outsmarted Dr. Snow," I said.

"A rock could outsmart Dr. Snow," whispered Dr. Clive. "He's book smart, but he doesn't have any common sense. I tried to warn him that this was a bad idea, but he wanted no part of it."

"He's the reason the others got out," Clive said. "*He* left the enclosure open! I don't know which I find more unbelievable: the fact that we cloned dinosaurs, or the fact that we were careless enough to let them escape."

Dad and I were hardly listening. We were both entranced by the Troodon.

"I love dinosaurs," he said. "Always have. The Troodon is miraculous. Some scientists theorize that if the dinosaurs hadn't died off, the Troodon would have evolved into a being with intelligence similar to that of humans."

"Humans?" I said.

"I've always thought they were more like birds than anything else. They just happened to have enormous brains," he said. "Now that I've actually seen them and looked them in the eye...if they'd had time to evolve another 70 million years or so, who knows? Maybe they'd be running this planet instead of us."

"Well, Dr. Clive, I think I should see one of these fellas in the wild, if I'm going to catch them," I said.

"That shouldn't be a problem. I know the perfect place," Dr. Clive said.

$ $ $

Moments later, we were waiting up in a lookout tower that Dr. Clive said was an old air signal tower, when Dad's cell phone rang. "It's Mom," he said.

Dr. Clive had already put out some meat in the field below us. He wanted to draw the Troodon out where I could see them.

Dad answered in a whisper. "Hi...I know it's late, honey," he said. "I'm not sure how much longer... you wouldn't believe me if I told you...I know he has school tomorrow...he's right here. Hold on."

I took the phone.

"Hi, Mom," I whispered.

"What are you guys doing? It's almost midnight," she asked.

"I know, Mom, but we're experiencing something that I can't really even believe is happening," I said. "I'll tell you all about it when I get home in the morning." She wasn't too happy about the fact that I was out so late, but she could tell it was important.

"Didn't you sign an agreement that you wouldn't tell anyone outside of the group about the dinosaurs?" Dr. Clive asked.

"Yes, but my mom doesn't count," I replied. "If you can't trust your mom, who can you trust?"

The Troodon appeared as if on cue. There were three of them. They gnawed on the meat and glanced cautiously around. More appeared slowly from the woods. Each one looked gray in the moonlight, stood about three feet tall, and looked like it had crawled right out of a sci-fi movie.

"That is officially the most amazing thing I've ever seen," I whispered to Dad, handing him his cell phone. He tried to take it, but must have lost his grip because it fell to the floor.

The noise startled the Troodon and, in an instant, they were gone.

"Now you see why catching them will be such a challenge," Dr. Clive said. "They're quick and smart. You've got your work cut out for you."

"Don't worry about it," I assured him. "No one will even know they were loose."

CHAPTER 8

The Daily Grind

Dad and I didn't get home until four in the morning. Still, I managed to drag myself to class.

"Someone looks tired," Mrs. Heart said, spotting me napping at my desk.

"I was up working on, uh..." I remembered my contract with the Institute. "A special project."

"You're too exhausted to learn," she said.

"I am!" I exclaimed. "In fact, I think I'd like to talk with the principal, Mrs. Heart. Can you please call down to her office and see if Mrs. Petty will meet me?"

Mrs. Heart looked shocked. She stared at me as if I had just said something in a foreign language that she didn't understand.

"What did you ask, Benji?" she said. "Are you sure you don't mean the nurse?"

"No, I'd like to see Mrs. Petty, the principal," I repeated. "Please."

"She's a busy woman, Benji," Mrs. Heart replied. "Students are usually not given the opportunity to simply stroll in and have a meeting."

"I realize that, and I mean no disrespect, Mrs. Heart," I continued. "But I'm going to need to see the principal."

The other kids were as confused as Mrs. Heart.

As far as I knew, a student at my school had never asked to sit down with the principal.

But, after a few moments, she agreed.

$ $ $

Ten minutes later, I returned to class with a note from the principal. The note informed Mrs. Heart that I was headed home early, and I'd be out for a few days. My classmates were stunned, but they weren't as shocked as my mother was when she arrived to pick me up.

"You must be so proud of Benji," the principal said to Mom, in the office.

"I'm very proud of him," Mom said, looking confused.

"First, the success of his app." Mrs. Petty was clearly working to fake a smile. "Which, I'll admit, is causing a lot of problems at the school, but at the same time raising some interesting conversations about honesty in the classroom."

"To be honest, I'm not a big fan of the app either," Mom added.

"But you must be so proud of his newest project!" Mrs. Petty exclaimed.

"I am," Mom said, looking confused. I knew Dad had told her about the Troodon after I left for school. "His father and I are very proud. It will be interesting to see how it all turns out. He's living a very exciting life these days."

"I think it's going to do a lot of good!"

"Well, we should get going," I said to Mom.

"I told Benji to take as many days as he needs for this project. Just keep us posted," said Mrs. Petty.

"I will," I promised. Mom and I walked out of the office. She didn't say a word until we got in the car and closed the doors.

"What was that all about?" she asked. "Your father said you guys signed a paper saying you wouldn't talk about the dinosaurs to anyone."

"Who said I mentioned anything about the dinosaurs to the principal?" I asked.

"You didn't make up some crazy excuse to get out of school did you?" questioned Mom.

"Nope, I told her the truth," I said.

"The whole truth?"

I cracked a small smile. "I just left out the parts about the dinosaurs."

I may also have mentioned something about making a sizeable donation to the school. How does the Benjamin "Benji" Franklin Mega Media Center sound?

CHAPTER 9
A Dino-Mite Plan!

Word spread quickly that I was working on a project at the old airport. The fact that trucks containing cows, chickens, and huge sheets of thick plastic were rolling through town may have helped. Our town is pretty small. Anytime something out of the ordinary happens, people know.

That afternoon, I met with Dr. Snow and Dr. Kent in a small office located near the hangar. Workers were assembling the high-security plastic into three large containers.

"When this thing's over, people will wonder what was going on back here," I said. "We'll have to work fast and get this done the first time. If everything goes as planned, I'll have the Troodon safely captured and loaded on a truck. You'll have to relocate them somewhere far from here."

"I already have a place lined up," Dr. Snow said. "It's perfectly safe, secure, and secluded."

"Fantastic!" I exclaimed. "By tomorrow morning, the town won't know any of this ever happened. Dr. Snow, if all goes as planned, I have one more thing I'm going to need from you guys."

"Anything, Benji," Dr. Snow agreed. "If you get us out of this dinosaur mess, you just say the word."

"I'll need you guys to give me the old airport," I told him. "In return, I'll donate funds to help you guys keep the Troodon out of trouble."

"No need for that, Benji," Dr. Kent said. "If you manage to save the day and recapture the Troodon safely, you'll have earned this airport." She reached out and shook my hand.

"What do you want the airport for?" Dr. Snow asked. "A personal jet?"

"No, I don't plan to do any flying," I said. (Besides, my own private jet was in the repair shop.)

"It'll be a gruesome scene if the Troodon attack the cows and chickens," Dr. Kent said, changing the subject.

"Don't worry about it," I said.

"What about all those cows and chickens?" Dr. Snow asked. "I think you may have gone a bit overboard on the bait. We've managed to lure the Troodon in with only a few steaks."

"You also haven't managed to catch them yet," I pointed out. "Just trust me."

$$\$\ \$\ \$$

The team and I worked all day setting up my plan. We built three large enclosures out of the thick, clear plastic. In one, we built a corral for the cows and in another a huge coop for the chickens. They were completely enclosed with the exception of airholes in the top. Nothing could get in or out.

The enclosures were placed right next to each other in the far field behind the old hangar.

The plastic was so clear that from a distance you couldn't see it at all.

In front of those enclosures, we placed the third. The third was identical to the other two, except the side facing the woods, where we knew the Troodon were hiding, was designed to be remotely lowered once they entered the structure.

The first part of my plan was that the Troodon would see and smell the cows and chickens. Once it was dark, they would come out of the woods to prey on the farm animals. They would mistakenly enter the empty container thinking they could reach the cows and chickens. But, when they were inside, I'd remotely close the fourth wall and capture them.

The plan was simple enough. If it worked, everyone would be amazed. I just had to pull it off without anything going wrong.

By the time night fell, everything was in place. There was only one thing left to do...

Find the Troodon.

The remote-control helicopter that I ordered had a night-vision camera mounted on the front. I flew it over the woods where we knew the Troodon were hiding.

"Do you think this will work?" Dad asked.

"I'm not sure," I said, concentrating on the remote. "But there's only one way to find out."

I flew the helicopter behind the Troodon. I didn't want them going in the opposite direction of the enclosure. They caught the scent of the cows and chickens because they were moving toward them. I followed close behind.

When the Troodon reached the edge of the woods, the dinos all stopped. I hovered above with the helicopter. The creatures seemed to be analyzing the situation. It was like a full buffet just waiting for them, but they were super cautious.

Over the course of an hour, the dinosaurs inched closer and closer toward the glass enclosure.

I was so afraid they would see their reflections and get spooked, but luckily that didn't happen. A cloudy sky hid the moonlight.

One after the other, the Troodon went inside. They walked to the far side of the enclosure thinking they'd be able to reach the cows and chickens.

Once they were all safely inside, I clicked the button and closed the enclosure with the fourth wall. *Yes!* I let out a sigh of relief, and Dr. Snow and his team cheered. For the first time since I'd met him, Dr. Clive smiled.

It worked like a charm. The Troodon were safely captured. We loaded the enclosure holding the dinosaurs onto a flat bed truck. Dr. Snow's team covered the beds with old semi trailers taken from grandpa's workshop.

Within a few hours, a truck bearing the logo "Ocean Wave Underwear" rolled out the front gate of the airport. The Troodon were on their way to a safe new location.

CHAPTER 10

Food for Thought

In the morning, I called Mom and told her to come out to the old airport. An hour later, I met her at the entrance.

Everyone else had gone with Dr. Snow to set up the Troodon in their new location. Dad and I had spent the night at the old airport and completed the second phase of my plan with the carpenters.

"How did it go last night?" Mom asked.

"You would have been very proud," Dad said. "Your son was like a hero without the cape and the silly suit."

"I can't say I'm surprised," she said. "He's always been brilliant."

"Thanks, Mom," I said. "But I have a surprise for you, too."

"You bought the dinosaurs as pets?" she asked.

"Haha. Funny, Mom," I said.

Dad and I climbed in her car and drove around to the back of the property, where the cows and chickens were located.

Overnight, Dad and I had released them into the field. It was completely fenced in, and they were free to roam. The main hangar was a perfect barn. The chickens were set up in the other hangar, which we turned into a giant chicken coop.

"I didn't know this was a farm. I thought it was all just abandoned," Mom said.

"It was, sort of. The cows and chickens are new. So are the two greenhouses," I said. The clear plastic enclosures made perfect greenhouses for growing crops.

"I don't get it," Mom said, puzzled. "What was the project you and your dad were working on up here? Where are the dinosaurs you told me about?"

"They're gone. Dr. Snow and his team are taking them somewhere safe," I explained, "In return for my help, I convinced them to give me all this land. I thought a farm might help solve the food shortage at the pantry. I think with all these cows and chickens your pantry will be sustainable now."

"What are you talking about, Benji?" Mom asked.

"Remember when you told me to let you know when I'd found a better way?" I asked. "I'm saying this farm is yours."

Mom opened her mouth to say something, but nothing came out. Instead, she gave me a hug.

"And I put several million dollars in an account," I said. "You can hire farmers to work the land and take care of the animals. You can buy trucks and staff to deliver the food. Whatever you need, I've got you covered."

"I don't know what to say," Mom exclaimed. "I'm amazed at what goes on in that brain of yours, Benjamin."

I thought about telling her that Troodon could be trained to make excellent pets. But I figured that could wait until after breakfast!

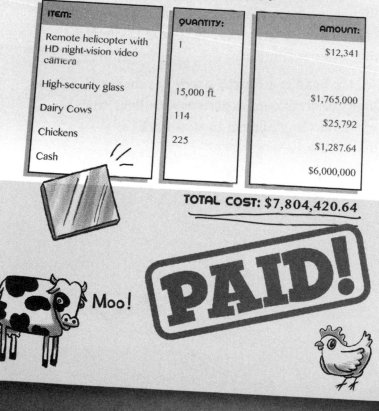

BADR INSTITUTE

NOTICE OF PAYMENT

FROM:
B.A.D.R. Institute

TO:
Benjamin "Benji" Franklin

PAYMENT DUE UPON RECEIPT

ITEM:	QUANTITY:	AMOUNT:
Remote helicopter with HD night-vision video camera	1	$12,341
High-security glass	15,000 ft.	$1,765,000
Dairy Cows	114	$25,792
Chickens	225	$1,287.64
Cash		$6,000,000

TOTAL COST: $7,804,420.64

Moo!

PAID!

RAYMOND BEAN

Raymond Bean is the best-selling author of the Sweet Farts and School Is A Nightmare series. His books have ranked #1 in Children's Humor, Humorous Series, and Fantasy and Adventure categories. He writes for kids that claim they don't like reading.

Mr. Bean is a fourth grade teacher with fifteen years of classroom experience. He lives with his wife and two children in New York.

Glossary

comprehend (kahm-pri-HEND)—to understand completely

controversial (kahn-truh-VUR-shuhl)—causing a great deal of disagreement

debris (duh-BREE)—the pieces of something that has been broken or destroyed

dire (DIRE)—dreadful or urgent

exploit (ek-SPLOIT)—to use something for your own advantage

guarantee (gar-uhn-TEE)—a promise that something will be done or will happen

holographic (huh-lah-GRAF-ick)—an image made by laser beams that looks as if it has depth and is three-dimensional

phase (FAZE)—a stage in the development of something

repelled (ri-PELD)—drove or pushed back

synapses (SIN-aps-iz)—the place where a signal passes from one nerve cell to another

viral (VY-ruhl)—quickly and widely spread

Million-Dollar Questions

1. Benji's mother and Mrs. Heart, his teacher, don't approve of the Excuse Yourself app he created. Do you think the app was appropriate? Why or why not?

2. Think of a time you used an excuse. Why did you use it? Did it work? How did you feel about making an excuse afterward?

3. Dr. Snow and the B.A.D.R. Institute asked biologists to clone the Troodon so that they could study it as paleontologists. What do you think are the benefits of cloning this dinosaur? What are the dangers?

4. Benji's tech class assignment is to create a computer app. Come up with your own idea for a computer app and explain how it could be used and who might use it.

5. Benji's mom doesn't approve of his Excuse Yourself app because she thinks it encourages people to lie. Do you think that coming up with excuses is the same as lying? Explain why or why not.

6. Imagine that Benji's plan doesn't work, and they can't capture the Troodon. Write a chapter explaining what happens.